Series consultant: Dr Terry Jennings

Designed by Jane Tassie

The authors and publisher would like to thank Lyn and Ken Edwards, Amit,
Troy and the staff and pupils of the Charles Dickens J & I School, London,
for their help in making this book.

A CIP record for this book is available from the British Library.

ISBN 0-7136-6195-X

First paperback edition published 2002
First published 1999 by A & C Black Publishers Limited
37 Soho Square, London W1D 3QZ
www.acblack.com

Typeset in 23/28pt Gill Sans Infant and 25/27 pt Soupbone Regular

Printed in Singapore by Tien Wah Press (Pte.) Ltd

A & C Black uses paper produced with elemental chlorine-free pulp,
harvested from managed sustainable forests.

Science Explorers

Wood

Exploring the science
of everyday materials

Nicola Edwards and
Jane Harris

Photographs by
Julian Cornish-Trestrail

A & C Black · London

Wood comes from trees.
It is used to make lots
of different things.
Look at all these
wooden objects
we've collected.

This pepper grinder feels hard and smooth.

3

These logs are heavy.

These twigs are dry and brittle.

This twig is light and springy.

I can bend it easily.

I can snap them in two!

These wooden objects come from different types of tree.

Look at all the colours!

6

We're arranging the objects from the lightest to the darkest.

There's a pattern in the wood.

My toy duck
has been carved
out of wood.
The wood has
been sanded
to make it
smooth.

It feels warm.

A pattern has been carved into this wooden printing block.

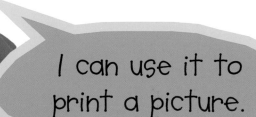

I can use it to print a picture.

My desk is made out of
seven pieces of wood
which have been nailed
together. The lid
is fixed with a
metal hinge.

I can open
and close it
easily.

This photo frame is made out of four pieces of wood. The pieces have been glued together.

Wood can be very strong.
Furniture is often made out
of wood. This wooden
chair is very sturdy.

It won't break . . .

. . . even if we
both sit on it!

This balsa wood is very light and bendy. It's good for making models.

Look at my plane fly!

13

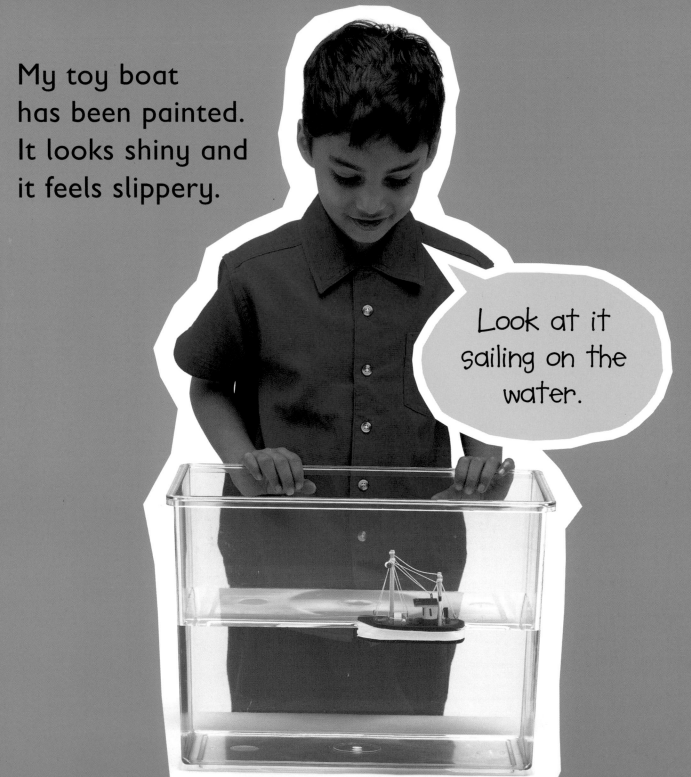

My toy boat
has been painted.
It looks shiny and
it feels slippery.

Look at it
sailing on the
water.

I wonder if my other
wooden toys will float.
Let's try them out.

15

These wooden bricks have got wet. The water has soaked into the wood.

The wood looks like it's changed colour.

These wooden bricks have been painted. They're wet too.

But the paint has stopped the water soaking into the wood.

I can see drops of water on top of the bricks.

I'm drawing a face. This stick of charcoal is made of burnt wood. The charcoal smudges very easily.

It makes my fingers all dirty!

Wood is made up of fibres which are used to make paper. I'm looking at paper through a magnifying glass.

These people are making paper. Look at the mixture being stirred and spread out to dry.

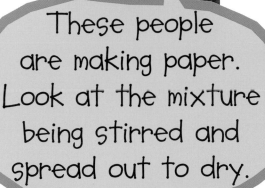

The mixture is called wood pulp. It contains fibres from wood.

21

Time to tidy away.
I've collected all
this paper for
recycling.

A lot of wood
is used to make
paper. We can
help to save
trees by
recycling
paper.

Notes for parents and teachers

The aim of the *Science Explorers* series is to introduce children to ways of observing and classifying materials, so that they can discover the various properties which make them suitable for a range of uses. By talking about what they already know about materials from their everyday use of different objects, the children will gain confidence in making predictions about how a material will behave in different circumstances. Through their explorations, the children will be able to try out their ideas in a fair test.

pp2/3, 12/13

Wood is one of our most valuable natural resources. There are two main types of wood, hardwoods (e.g. oak and elm) and softwoods (e.g. pine and larch). Hardwoods come from broad-leaved trees. Most have beautiful grain patterns and are often used for making ornaments, furniture and flooring. Softwoods generally come from evergreen, cone-bearing trees. They are used for building and to make wood pulp for making paper. Point out to the children that the terms hardwood and softwood do not indicate the hardness of wood (balsa wood, for example, comes from a hardwood tree).

Ask the children to think of everyday things which are made from wood. How would those things be different if they were made from other materials? What are the advantages of them being made from wood?

pp4/5

The bark on the outside of a tree protects the growing wood. A new layer of wood grows each year, making the tree thicker and stronger. If possible, show the children a tree trunk or a log with the rings clearly visible. Can they work out the age of the tree?

Wood contains a lot of water. Branches and twigs that still contain water will be soft and bendy. Older, dried-out branches will be brittle and easy to snap. If you can take the children for a walk around a wooded area, ask them to listen out for the sound of wood snapping under their feet.

pp6/7

Some trees, such as beech and maple, produce wood that is very pale, while others such as mahogany and walnut, produce a rich, dark wood. Each type of wood also has a distinguishable grain pattern. The patterns within the grain are influenced by the rate at which the tree grows. In general, hardwoods grow more slowly than softwoods and produce more beautiful grain patterns.

pp8/9

Show the children a range of carved wooden objects. Try to include a variety of new and old objects. What do the objects feel like? Do the older objects feel different to the newer ones? Compare the use of wooden printing blocks with other ways of printing a pattern, such as with the use of rubber stampers.

pp10/11

Investigate the different methods of joining wood. If possible, visit a building site to see how the timber frame of a house is constructed. Think about the other parts of the house which will be made of wood, such as the doors, stairs and floors. Discuss how the pieces of wood used to make them will be joined together.

pp14/17

Paint and varnish prevent damage to wood from insects and fungi and protect it from wet weather. Show the children some rotting wood. What does the wood feel and smell like? Are there insects or fungi living inside it? When unprotected wood gets wet, it absorbs water. The unpainted bricks shown on pages 16/17 will be heavier than the painted bricks, as they have absorbed water. The children could investigate this by weighing unpainted and unvarnished bricks before and after they have been soaked in water.

pp18/19

Wood for a bonfire needs to be old and dry so that it will catch light easily. What do the children think would happen if the wood was wet? Can they describe the sounds, smells and colours of a bonfire? Why do the children think many residential areas have banned the use of wood-burning fires?

pp22/23

Talk to the children about the effects of deforestation, in our own country as well as in the tropics where whole rainforests are being chopped down. Discuss ways to help save trees, e.g. by not wasting paper, by collecting paper for recycling and by using products made from recycled paper.

Find the page

Here is a list of some of the words and ideas in this book